SATURDAY SHILLINGS

Antelope Books

Saturday Shillings

PENELOPE FARMER

Illustrated by

PRUDENCE SEWARD

HAMISH HAMILTON
LONDON

First published in Great Britain 1965
by Hamish Hamilton Ltd.
90 Great Russell Street, London, WC1B 3PT
Second impression 1966
Third impression 1966
Fourth impression 1968
Fifth impression 1970
Sixth impression 1972
Seventh impression 1975

SBN 241 91176 1

PRINTED PHOTOLITHO IN GREAT BRITAIN
BY EBENEZER BAYLIS AND SON, LTD.
THE TRINITY PRESS, WORCESTER, AND LONDON

CONTENTS

1

Morning

IT was Saturday morning and the sun was back at last after a week of rain. When Peter began his breakfast the sun just splashed the edge of the sink. By the time he was finished, it had crept across the kitchen to the table and a tongue of it lay warm on his plate. It made him feel happier. To please his mother he drank back a whole mug of milk. He waited till, sighing, she had folded her crackly newspaper. Only then did he ask, carefully and anxiously:

"Have you any jobs for me today, Mummy?" She paid him a shilling for each job he did properly. Not for jobs like washing-up and making his bed, which he had to do anyway, but for extra jobs like weeding the garden.

"I should think so, love," she said. "There's always something needs doing."

"*Lots* of jobs?" asked Peter hopefully. But he felt his face turning warm and red.

"Peter's gone all red," his younger sister Lucy said. "Mummy, just look." She had tight fat plaits with sticking-out ends like toothbrushes, and Peter longed to tug at one. But that would only make his mother cross.

"Lucy, you just shut *up*," he said.

"*Lots* of jobs, Peter?" his mother asked. "How many do you mean?"

Peter dared not look at her but he could feel her eyes on him. He pushed his knife round and round his plate for something to do.

"Well—f-fifteen jobs, p'raps, or—or—nineteen—or twenty. *Lots* of jobs. You know, Mum."

"*Twenty* jobs?" asked Lucy, making her eyes round as peppermints.

"*Twenty* jobs?" asked his mother. "Why Peter—haven't you tried to earn any of that pound yet at *all*?"

Peter tapped on his plate with the knife. Without thinking he tapped a tune.

"N-no," he said miserably.

"And it has to be in by tonight?"

"Yes," he said.

"How long ago were you told about this camp, Peter?" his mother asked.

"Three—no four weeks," he mumbled.

"And what did I say when you asked to go?"

Peter grew cross. She knew the answers to her questions as well as he did. His tap-

ping changed to a hard drum tapping, no tune at all, tap! tap! *tap!*

He said, "You told me I'd have to earn my own fare this time."

"Yes. And why?"

"Because it'd be the third camp I'd been on this summer and I couldn't always expect to be given everything."

"And isn't that fair?" she asked.

"Yes," muttered Peter, but he did not

think so. He drove his knife so hard against his plate that Lucy squealed, "You'll *break* it, Peter." But his mother just went on looking at him.

"You *silly* old Peter. I'd have given you a job whenever you asked, only you never did. What about your pocket-money? Haven't you saved any of that?"

"No." For he had spent it all on sweets and pistol caps with his friend Thomas and the other boys. Four weeks before it had not seemed so difficult to earn a pound. He was always sure he could earn it by doing jobs for his mother. And he had thought that perhaps if he was lucky he might even earn it all at once with a reward for finding a dog or a diamond brooch. Or by winning a competition in a comic or on the back of a cornflakes packet. Some people did. But he had not found any dogs or brooches and he had forgotten to keep the comics and the cornflake packets. And each day he had said to himself, "I'll start earning it tomorrow." Only he never had started.

That morning all he had in the world was sixpence. But if he did not hand in a whole pound to the headmaster by seven o'clock that evening the camp bus would be off next week-end without him.

"Please, Mummy," he said miserably, "please, Mummy, I'd do all jobs specially well, honest I would . . . honest cater-pillars."

His mother looked away out of the window, thinking. Peter had stopped even tapping with his knife. His hands waited, still and anxious as the rest of him.

But when she turned back to him at last she said, quite gently, "No, Peter, *no* I'm sorry. I can't give you twenty jobs today. I'll give you two, but you'll just have to find the rest for yourself if you can. It's your own fault for being such a silly and leaving it so late."

"Oh, Mummy!" Peter was horrified. He had been so certain that through her it would all come right.

But his mother was shaking all the egg-shells on to a plate and bundling together the cornflake spoons and her face did not look any more helpful or comforting to Peter than the dirty cups and plates on the table.

But after all, what she did was kind. She took no notice when Peter sulked and banged about the kitchen. She told him he need not help with the dishes today, and the jobs she gave him were quick easy ones that she knew he liked doing.

First he had to bring in wood for the fire. It had been such a cold July that they had been glad of a fire in the evenings. Although it was sunny today his mother said you could never trust the weather now, and better be prepared. Peter thought she chose it as the quickest job she could think of for him. But he did not want to be grateful.

His father would have finished in two minutes by filling the wood-basket outside and carrying it all into the sitting-room at once. Peter was not strong enough for that, he had to bring the wood in armfuls to put in the basket where it lived beside the fire. Even that did not take long, though in his hurry he tried to carry too much, and two great logs fell from the top of his pile and left scrapings of bark and wood-dust on the carpet. He would have kicked the mess under a chair only his mother came in and sent him for a dust-pan to sweep it up. But bark still

clung to his shirt where he had clutched the peeling wood against him.

Then he was given his favourite job, cleaning the bath. Peter usually spent a long time at this. He would flood the bath with a great sweep of water and let it suck back, sudden as the sea tide. And then he would dam it with a cloth so that there was a lake at one end of the bath and only a thinning trickle of water in the rest.

But today it shone all over in ten minutes and Peter was running down the path with the comforting feel of two silver shillings banging in his pocket. Which was better than the same pocket's emptiness straight after breakfast.

At the bottom of the path he slowed, and a kind of lump seemed to settle inside him. He had been too busy before to think about it. Or rather he had not wanted to think and it had been easy not to. But now he had to think and he realized he did not know where to start looking for work. He opened the gate slowly, pulling the catch up with his hand, and not letting it spring back as it usually did. As if that would make a spell to help him.

With half his mind he saw standing in

the road outside, the small blue car belonging to Mr. Johnson from next door. There was mud along its sides. Just as Peter finished shutting the gate Mr. Johnson himself came out and smiled at him. Mr. Johnson was a very tidy-looking man. When he smiled he parted his teeth as neatly as he parted his hair. His voice was tidy too, but tried to burst out in a jolly way for Peter.

"And how are you, Peter, this lovely morning? Glad of the sun I expect. Off to play cricket, eh?"

"No," said Peter. "I'm very well, thank you," he added, in case that had sounded rude. Because, after all, it was not Mr. Johnson's fault that he could not play cricket today.

"Good lad," said Mr. Johnson, "good lad." He climbed into his car and started the engine. The little blue car growled and leapt away, but it left Peter with an idea.

He set off, half running down the road,

keeping his eyes carefully to the ground so that he would not give himself bad luck by stepping on the lines. And so that he would not miss a sixpence or a diamond brooch that someone might have dropped.

The mud on the car had reminded him how his friends in London used to earn five shillings a time for cleaning cars. And why should he not do the same? The church clock rang out ten times as he ran. He counted the strikes. Ten o'clock!

"Five shillings . . . five shillings . . ." Peter stopped his feet so that he could concentrate on adding up with his fingers. That meant he would only have to clean . . . four cars, and then he would have his pound and some over with the money his mother had given him.

Surely on a Saturday morning four people would want their cars cleaned? The lump went away from inside him. Everything seemed easy again, and joyfully he jumped from square to square. But still he kept his eyes on the ground and so bumped straight into someone coming along the pavement.

"Mind out where you're going," a voice said. And Peter saw Mr. Richards standing there. He threw his eyes back to the ground and dared not be the first to move. Peter did not like Mr. Richards. He did not like him because he was frightened of him. A lot of the children in the village were frightened of him too. He lived by himself in the largest house in Peter's road and never visited anyone in the village or asked them to visit him.

The children whispered that he was mean, a miser, or even worse. They called him Old Dicky, and the worst dare to give anyone was to send them to steal a flower or a weed or a stone from Old Dicky's garden.

Yet it was not that he looked so very

frightening. Peter sometimes wondered why he frightened them all so much. He was rather like one of the herons at the pond where Peter went fishing. He was so tall and thin that none of his clothes seemed quite big enough for him. The strangest thing about him was that though he did not appear especially cross or miserable he never smiled. He stood now, looking down at Peter, neither angry nor friendly.

"You'd better mind out," he said again. He always leant his voice heavily on the end of his sentences. "You could cause an *accident*."

"I'm sorry, sir," Peter said. Usually he would have run on as soon as he could. But today looking round he saw Mr. Richards' car standing outside his garage. And it was very dirty. His eagerness came back to him. It jumped over his fear in a leap. His voice burst out, without him being able to hold it back.

"Can I clean your car, sir?" He felt very brave as he said that.

Mr. Richards as usual did not frown with his face. But his voice frowned.

"Are you being cheeky?"

All Peter's fear returned. He wished he could take his boldness back again.

"N-no, sir," he said. "H-honestly—I just thought."

"I am well aware that my car is dirty," Mr. Richards said.

"I'm sorry, I-I didn't mean . . ." said Peter changing feet backwards and for-wards.

"Keep *still* can't you? All right, my car needs cleaning. You clean it. And mind you do it *properly*."

Mr. Richards' car was very dirty. It was

an old Ford and the dirt and dust seemed
to have grown on it like moss, or even to
have been stuck on with glue. No matter
how hard Peter scrubbed he could not
make it come off. He could not make the
surface shine.

Great muddy splashes joined the wood-
dust on his shirt. Though the sun, for
July, was not especially hot he began to

feel as if he was working among furnaces in an engine room. He felt as if he was a furnace himself, as if his scrubbing arms were driven by fire or steam. Only the thought of his five shillings wage kept him at work, and that did not seem nearly enough money for this. Sometimes Mr. Richards came out to look at him, and went away without a word.

When Peter had been to empty Mr. Richards' yellow bucket for the fourth time he stopped and stood back from the car. He looked at it, hating it, hating Mr. Richards, hating everything. It would have to do, he thought. It had taken him hours and hours, he had never worked so hard in his life. If it wasn't clean now that was Mr. Richards' fault for letting it get so dirty.

He took the torn old piece of cloth Mr.

Richards had given him and wrung it out
in the clean water. He rubbed it once more
all over the car, trying not to see the dusty
runnels and smears in every piece of mould-
ing and in every angle. Then he went and
knocked on the back door as Mr. Richards
had told him to do.

"All right," said Mr. Richards' voice almost before Peter's hand had dropped back, "all right." The door opened so sud-

denly that Peter, easily frightened here, jumped back in fright.

Mr. Richards stood on the door-mat wearing an apron. Unlike the rest of his clothes which always seemed too short, this was too long for him.

"Finished?" he asked.

"Mm," said Peter, wishing he had polished over the car just one more time.

"I'll come and see if you've done it properly."

But he stood looking at the car so long Peter almost thought he had forgotten him. Mr. Richards' face said nothing. His long hands played with the apron strings, pulling them tight and then loose again, making the folds of cloth round his waist shift and change.

"Hm," he said at last, "and what do you charge for *that*?"

Peter hesitated a long moment. He was hot and miserable, the morning was slipping away, and he had done little to earn his money. He was cross with Mr. Richards for his dirty car, cross with himself because he knew that he had not done the job properly. And he knew what his mother would have said to that.

Five shillings was the wage he had meant to ask. That was what his friends in London had earned for each car they cleaned. But suddenly it seemed to Peter a lot of money. Especially when he looked and saw the dust still caught in the corners of the Ford car. He wondered if he dared ask Mr. Richards for as much money as that.

But all the time he had been cleaning the car it was only the thought of the five shillings that had kept him at work. Besides now he was so hot and cross that he would almost have dared to do anything. And besides, Mr. Richards with an apron round his waist seemed less frightening than the usual Mr. Richards, without one.

So Peter gulped a little and said: "F-five shillings. F-five shillings I think." But his voice wobbled as much as the see-saw in the school yard.

"Five *shillings*?" Mr. Richards hissed, soft as a snake. "*Five* shillings?" This time he bellowed. Peter had not known he would bellow so loud. "Are you joking?"

"No," said Peter miserably. He had not been joking but now, apron or not, he was so frightened of Mr. Richards he dared not lie about that. He wished he could be running away down the road with no wage at all, anything to escape from Old Dicky.

"Old Dicky, Dicky, Dick," he said in his mind to make him feel better. "Silly old

Dicky, why should I be frightened of you?" But he was.

"And he calls that car *clean*." Mr. Richards seemed to be talking to himself. His hand went to his pocket, it fumbled there a minute and something chinked under the apron folds. Then his hand appeared again holding something out into the air, not for or at Peter, just into empty air.

"Take it," he said impatiently. "Take

it." Peter hesitated between Mr. Richards' voice and his hand held out to nobody.

"Take it, that's all you're worth, that's *all*." And when Peter fumblingly had got the coins into his hand he turned away and shut the door behind him, his face as usual showing nothing at all.

Peter found himself walking down the road. His hand was in his pocket clutching the two shillings from his mother and the two sixpences from Mr. Richards. Three shillings it made altogether. And at that moment the church clock struck again and this time he counted eleven strokes one after another. Eleven o'clock and he had earned three shillings precisely, and no more.

He trudged down the road, hot, aching and miserable, not sure even where he was going. A bicycle bell behind him made him jump and he turned to find his friend Thomas there. Thomas was the only person Peter had told about having to earn the money. But he never remembered anything.

"Coming to play, Peter?" he called, flying past easy as an aeroplane, it seemed to the trudging Peter. Lucky, lucky Thomas flying on his bicycle. But Peter had to shake his head, kicking at the pavement.

"You *know* I can't come," he said crossly.

" 'Course," said Thomas. "Sorry." He waved and was gone. He did not seem to care.

Oh, how unfair everything was this morning, Peter thought. He kicked his toes against the pavement and clenched his hands in his pockets.

But that was, after all, the worst of the morning. Just a minute later he saw Mr. Harris blinking over his fence at the sun. Peter liked Mr. Harris. Most people did.

He hesitated a moment and then asked politely, "Please, Mr. Harris, please, sir, have you any jobs I could do?"

Mr. Harris never used more words than

he had to. He smiled and said, "Let's see, my car needs a clean."

Peter hesitated again. After Mr. Richards'

he was not sure he ever wanted to clean another car. But it seemed silly to say no.

In fact, compared to Mr. Richards' car Mr. Harris' looked clean before he started. Moreover Mr. Harris had a hose which he let Peter use. Holding it, letting the jet of water climb and fall against the car, Peter felt like a fireman. He rinsed off the soap in waterfalls and the whole car seemed to glitter and move with water under the sun.

Polishing was hard hot work again. But Mr. Harris brought him out lemonade to drink, and gave him a leather which made the work easier. Peter rubbed till he could see his face everywhere. It looked swollen as if he had mumps where the wings of the car curved round. Among the cracks and corners it looked all dented and twisted.

Afterwards Mr. Harris seemed pleased and asked Peter what he charged for the job. Peter turned red, redder than he had with the work. He stood on one foot and rubbed the back of his leg with the other, and chinked the money in his pocket.

"Two shillings? Would that be all right?" he asked anxiously at last.

"That's not much for a good job of work," said Mr. Harris, and gave him

half-a-crown. Peter had the sad feeling
that Mr. Harris would gladly have given
him five shillings, had he dared ask. But
perhaps it would have been greedy to ask
for so much. And the fat half-crown felt
rich among the shillings and sixpences in
his pocket.

By lunch-time his earnings had risen to
seven shillings and sixpence. No one else,
to his relief, had wanted their car cleaned,

but he had walked one dog and brushed another. He had only earned sixpence for the brushing because the dog had wriggled like a worm and Peter could not brush it at all. After a little while its mistress had told Peter that perhaps he had better stop. But she said it nicely and anyway the clock was striking again, and Peter was almost late home for dinner.

"Well?" asked Lucy as soon as he had shut the back door behind him. "How much have you earned?"

"Oh lots," said Peter carelessly.

He would have been too proud to say anything else now. Yet it did seem true that he was doing well. He had almost forgotten Mr. Richards. He had done a good hard morning's work. And the seven-and-sixpence he had earned was after all quite a lot of money. Eight shillings it made with his pocket-money sixpence.

At least it seemed a lot as long as he did not think about the twelve shillings still to be earned before seven o'clock. But there were sausages for dinner and lemon curd pudding, almost his favourite foods. So it was easy enough for him to think about the seven-and-six he had earned, rather than the twelve shillings still to be found. He thought hard about the seven-and-six, and with that and the sausages and the lemon curd, he seemed so happy that Lucy said, "Mummy, I think Peter's having a lovely time doing jobs. Why can't I go

too? I'd earn him lots and lots of money."

Her mother smiled at the horror on Peter's face.

"Of course you can't go Lucy. Peter wants to earn it himself. You wait till you're a little older."

2

Afternoon

BUT after lunch, walking down the path, Peter was not happy any more. The twelve shillings began to seem more important than the seven-and-sixpence. And he did not know where to start looking for more jobs. All he knew was that he did not want to clean any more cars today.

His friends in London had sometimes gone round knocking on doors and asking for work. But it was different here in a village where most people knew who you were, and might disapprove unless it was something official like bob-a-jobbing. Besides, it was easy to be brave if you were with someone else. Even in London Peter was not sure that he would have had the courage to face those blind front doors on his own.

He looked down the road to see if that would give him an idea again. No one was there. Nothing moved but a black and

white dog sniffing the fence by Mr. Richards' garden. Even the dog moved slowly and lazily in the sun, as if it only sniffed there because it had nothing better to do, not because Mr. Richards' fence smelt better than any other.

Perhaps it was lost, Peter thought hopefully for a minute. Perhaps he might get some money as a reward for finding it. But the dog did not look very lost. And after a minute a voice called it from the end of the road and it jerked up its head and ran off.

Since there was nothing else to help Peter down the road, he looked up the road instead. Their house was at the end of the row and the row was at the very edge of the village. So the pavements stopped and the road went on between banks and hedges and fields up to a crest of hill, then over and down again to a wood and a stream and two ponds linked together on the stream like stones on a necklace. You could not see all that from here but Peter went fishing so often with Thomas that he could see them now in his mind.

At the crest of the hill was a gate. It led from the road into a field of fruit bushes that stood in lines like bushy soldiers. By the gate was a board nailed to a post. From here it was just a dark shape up against the sky. But Peter knew that when you got nearer the board said, in black letters faded to grey,

Private Property
Stephen's Fruit Farm
TRESPASSERS KEEP OUT

Seeing the dark shape of the board on

49

the hill's crest he remembered what he had only ever half-noticed before—sometimes pinned over the faded letters was a piece of paper asking for fruit or potato pickers.

Perhaps there would be a piece of paper now. At least it was worth going to have a look. He had to think things out and he could be thinking just as easily while he

walked up the hill as he could standing here by the gate. Walking might even help him to think, he decided.

But he did not walk—he ran up the hill. As he drew nearer the top he could see there was something pinned to the board, a piece of paper. One drawing pin had come out and the corner moved gently as if it was alive.

Peter ran faster, and fell on the gate panting.

The piece of paper said: "Fruit pickers wanted. Good rates paid." That was printed neatly in ink. Underneath was scribbled more roughly in pencil, "Black-currant-picking in progress now."

Peter gazed at it, hardly daring to believe what he saw. But after a moment he shook himself and went through the gate, carefully pulling it to behind him. He had

fumbled in his hurry to open the gate and
get to work but now he saw backs hunched
and bent over the bushes further down the
field. Just off the track nearby a small
truck was standing with two men leaning

against it, puffing at pipes. Even though Peter wanted the job so badly he suddenly felt shy, and he placed the hook carefully and slowly in the chain which held the gate shut to delay things a moment. Then he walked up the rutted, empty track and the two men turned to watch him come.

"What do you want?" one of them shouted.

Peter stopped and watched them. He made his hands into fists at his sides, and his voice sounded thin in the open air.

"The notice—I saw the notice."

"Well?" asked the man who had shouted.

"I-I thought I might pick fruit for you."

The man did a great laugh like a bear. "You're a bit young aren't you? How old are you?"

"I'm nine," Peter said indignantly. "And

I've often picked blackcurrants. We've got six blackcurrant bushes in our garden."

"Well we've got a good sight more than that here," said the man.

So far the other man had puffed at his pipe, and said nothing. But now he turned to fumble in the back of the truck and brought out a white fruit basket like the

punnets Peter's mother used, only bigger.

"It won't do the lad any harm to try," he said, and held the basket out to Peter.

The first man frowned. "All right," he said. "But the first time I see you eating, OUT you go. And mind you pick carefully. You can't sell squashed currants, so if you don't pick carefully you won't get paid."

The second man was kinder. He smiled at Peter, round his pipe. "It's not so bad," he said. "And it's a shilling for each basket you fill." He pointed to a row of bushes. "You get started on those and we'll see how you do." He smiled again and made his pipe smoke curl into the air.

As he picked his way over the field, holding his basket carefully, Peter stared at the other pickers. They were all women, and mostly fat. They reminded him a little of the Mrs. Noah from Lucy's Noah's Ark. They talked to each other, odd words thrown out at a time, but their eyes never moved from the blackcurrant bushes, not even to look at the stranger, Peter. Their hands moved swiftly as if they were milking cows, but instead of white milk streaming into buckets, the dark currant clusters popped steadily into the white fruit baskets.

Peter found it was quite different from picking his mother's fruit. She had one row of currants, and beyond, another taller row of raspberries. The wire fruit cage shut you in all round and you could see the house just a little way up the garden.

But here the bushes stretched endlessly like the pictures of Australia in the geography book, Peter thought. There was nothing to see but bushes. The sun beat down on his back but round his feet the field earth was churned and muddy from

the rain and the mud hung in clods to his shoes.

The currants were not easy to find. They hid behind spiked and knobbly twigs, behind thick dusty leaves. Peter's fingers groped for them slowly, but at first he did not mind. He was even enjoying it and hummed softly to himself.

But after he had picked for what seemed a long while and all the women nearby had filled their baskets and fetched new ones, and almost filled those he began to grow worried. For at the bottom of his basket there was still only a small layer of fruit. He had to fill twelve baskets if he was going to earn all the money he needed. However was he going to do that, if he was so slow to fill one?

He began to try to make his hands move faster, like the other pickers, the Noah's Ark women. At first, remembering what the fierce bear man had told him, he had been very slow and careful, much slower than when he picked for his mother. But now his hands began to tear the fruit from the bushes. Leaves, twigs, currants alike went tumbling into his basket, and the currants squashed beneath his fingers, staining them purple.

His back began to ache. His feet were caked with the dragging mud. His fingers were sore with the spikes of the currant bushes. And still his basket was not nearly

full. Peter did not hum to himself any more.

Then, suddenly, he noticed that he had come almost to the end of a row of bushes, right up to the hedge itself. It was too high here for him to see over the top. But if he put his face close up to it he could see through a thorny gap into the lane.

If only, Peter thought . . . if only he was out there again in the lane, free to look for other, better jobs. This currant picking was no good at all. He wished he had never begun.

As he peered out a bicycle came up the hill. He saw its front wheel first and two hands on the handlebars. Then all the bicycle and its rider came in sight. The rider was a boy about Peter's size and quite suddenly he saw it was Thomas,

with a fishing-net sticking up behind him
like a flag and an empty jam-jar dangling
from his handlebars. The hill was so steep
here that to move at all he had to stand
upright on the pedals and push them down
with all his might, puffing and panting
like a steam-engine. The nearer he came

to Peter the slower he went, till he was almost standing still. His legs heaved down like pistons, his puffed-out cheeks were red as pillar-boxes.

Peter, giggling, forgot about fruit-picking. Just as Thomas came level with his peephole he threw a handful of currants at him.

Thomas was startled. He wobbled, grabbed, and wobbled again. The bicycle came to a dead stop and Thomas at last fell off, though not hard enough to hurt. He picked himself and the bicycle up off the ground and stood twisting himself

round like a corkscrew to see where the currants had come from.

"Hey," he said, "stop it whoever you are. Ambushes aren't *fair*." Then he saw Peter's giggling face mixed up in the hedge. He was too surprised to remember to be cross about falling off.

"Whatever are you doing in *there*, Peter?" he asked.

"I've got a job. I'm currant-picking." Peter was proud of it for a moment.

"Any good?" asked Thomas.

"Well . . ." Peter looked down at his half-empty basket, "not *very* good. I'm quite good at cleaning cars though," he boasted, "some cars anyway——" For suddenly he remembered Mr. Richards' Ford.

"Well I'm Pedro the fisherman," Thomas said. "Coming?"

"I *can't* . . ." Peter began. Then he looked back at his basket. It looked emptier than ever. And now also he noticed how squashed the topmost currants were, because he had picked them in such a hurry.

He remembered again the bear man telling him to be careful. He did not like the thought of showing him the fruit. He wondered if any wages would be worth the trouble he might get into for squashing the currants so badly. He did not want more trouble like the trouble he had had with Mr. Richards in the morning.

How hot and scratched and tired he felt. He thought of the soft cool water at the bottom of the hill, and the darting, tiny fish. Never in Peter's life had the thought of fishing seemed so good.

Surely it would not hurt to go, just for

five minutes? After all he had worked very hard the whole morning.

"Snail-thinker," Thomas said. "I'm not going to wait till the end of the world."

Peter found that he could not bear Thomas to go without him. "Wait for me, I'm Pedro the second. I'm coming."

He put his basket down on the ground and glanced round cautiously. But no one seemed interested in him. The Noah's Ark women were still bent over their bushes. The nice man was far away over the other side of the field. There was no sign of the fierce bear man at all.

Peter bent himself double like a fish-hook, and crept up the field between the bushes and the hedge, as fast as he dared. But not too fast, in case someone saw him and called him back. On and on he crept

until at last, panting, he had reached the topmost bush, by the track .

He peered round it. Still no one seemed to have noticed him. Just to show he did not care about the bear man, he grabbed two currants off the bush and ate them. They tasted sour to his mouth as he flung himself on to the track, racing for the gate.

Again he fumbled to undo the hook and chain. They seemed to be glued together. He dared not look behind him. But no shouts came from the field, no bear-like bellowings. And then he was through, and free and safe at last between the tall hedges of the lane.

Thomas waited a little way up the lane, grinning at Peter. He was balanced on his bicycle again, one foot on the road, the other on the pedal, ready to push himself away down the hill.

"Right," he said, "all aboard the flying saucer."

Peter put his leg over the carrier and held on to the saddle. The iron carrier bit

into the skin of his legs, the saddle springs bit at his fingers, and then Thomas pushed once on the pedals and they were away.

Work, jobs, earnings—fell from Peter's back like great bundles. The wind grazed his face, and blew his shirt into a cool fan. For a moment he forgot everything but this flying down the hill on a bicycle.

"That was *super*," he said to Thomas at the bottom of the hill.

He had truly meant to fish for only five minutes. His need to earn the money weighed as heavy on him as ever, when he let himself think about it. But somehow, when one fish had been caught he had to catch another. And when the jar was full and Peter began to think about work again, two coots started to fight.

Thomas and Peter froze still, watching. The coots butted out their bare white

heads. They jumped in the air, their wings stretched out, and bumped their breasts together. Sometimes they chased each other with strange, rough calls and cries. Peter and Thomas each chose one to support. They muttered "come on, boy" under their breaths, like people at boxing matches.

But suddenly the church clock sounded from over the hill.

At first stroke Peter jerked alive, forgetting the coots. He held his breath and counted.

A second stroke came. Two.

A third, three. And then, in horror, he could hardly believe it, a fourth stroke sounded. Four o'clock! It was no good asking Thomas to lend his bike. Thomas never lent it to anyone. So Peter ran. He ran back up the hill which he had flown down before. It was much steeper than the hill up the other side from his house.

His lungs burst. His legs cracked. Towards the top he worked harder and

harder to go slower and slower, like Thomas had on his bicycle. He went slower than a walk. Until he came to the top at last and ran over and down and free again.

But he did not have time to think how

tired he was. All the time the thought beat at him, that by seven o'clock he still had to find twelve shillings. Since dinner-time he had earned nothing at all.

Things were desperate now. He must not mind what people would say. He must knock on doors and ask for work as if he was doing a bob-a-job for the Cubs. Even so he did not dare go where he lived and was known, but ran on to the far side of the village to start. And by the time he reached there it was getting on for half past four.

3

Evening

SOME people looked cross and said, No, not even thank you, as Peter stood hopefully on their doorsteps. Some slammed doors in his face. But there were others who welcomed his help.

Between half past four and six o'clock he weeded two flower-beds, mowed a very small lawn, and took in a lineful of washing. He also minded a baby for five minutes while its mother ran to the shops. The baby, luckily, stayed sleeping, and Peter took the chance to rest, and to eat a

rather soft humbug he found stuck to the lining of his pocket.

He ached all over with work. But he could not keep up with the beating, heart-less clock. At six o'clock he was in the middle of scrubbing out a large cupboard. As quarter past six sounded he finished the cupboard and was given a shilling for wages. But still no more than thirteen shillings lay in his pocket. And still he had seven whole shillings to earn.

Suddenly all Peter's luck seemed gone. Even clouds gathered thick over the sun. Two doors were slammed in his face. Half past six rang out and he found himself trudging, heavily, at the bottom of his own road. Every bit of him ached. He could feel his back, his legs, his feet. His hands pricked and his face still felt hot with sun. For the first time he completely

gave up hope. He would not be going to camp.

All day he had said to himself, I'm going to camp, I'm going to go. He had never let himself doubt that he would earn the money in the end. But he could not say that any more. There was only half an hour left till seven o'clock. He could not earn seven shillings in half an hour. Even if he found a dog or a brooch that someone had lost he would not get the reward in time. Anyway he did not believe in dogs and brooches any more. Only a miracle now would make it possible for him to go.

"It's not *fair*, it's not *fair*," he repeated to himself. He ran over the day in his mind. If only he had not gone fishing with Thomas, if only he had not wasted time in the blackcurrant field, wasted time cleaning Mr. Richards' car. He plodded hopelessly along and then, for the second time that day, he bumped into someone.

"And where would you be going?" the voice asked above his head.

"Sorry," said Peter, and would have walked on. But suddenly he realized that it was Mr. Richards who again stood in his way, and that he could not go without

bumping into him. He waited looking at Mr. Richards' feet, waiting for them to move.

"Still *working*?" asked Mr. Richards' voice after a long while. And before Peter could reply he asked, "Want another job?"

Peter began to shake his head. It was too late now, he could never earn enough to pay his fare, least of all from mean Mr. Richards. He just wanted to go home and forget all about work and camp and earnings.

But then he looked again at Mr. Richards' white and thin unsmiling face. It waited there above his tall thin body in the dull evening light. Peter remembered the children's whispering and he was afraid. "Old Dicky, Dicky, Dick," he said to himself again, but it did not help at all. He was frightened.

"Want another job?" asked Mr. Richards for a second time, and scratched his ear with a long white hand. Peter dared not say No. He dared not even speak but just nodded his head.

"Right," said Mr. Richards. "You can get going on my rose-bed. I'll pay what it's worth when you've finished."

His rose-bed needed weeding quite as badly as his car had needed cleaning. Peter crouched over it with a trowel, and a basket beside him to put the weeds in. He felt so tired that he worked like a machine, not like a boy, digging the weeds out, throwing them into the basket.

Over and over him ran the thought of the camp. He thought of telling his mother that he could not go. She would be kind, not cross, he knew, and that would make it worse. But he could imagine what Lucy would say. And the boys at school. How could he tell them? They had thought he was coming, they would want to know now why he was not. But he could never tell them why.

"It's not *fair*, it's not *fair*," he growled to himself. It was his mother's fault. None of the other boys had to pay for themselves, why should he? He pulled the weeds out of the earth and tossed them into the basket as if they were his enemies.

But he knew it was fair really. He could have earned the money if he had tried before. It was all his own fault for leaving it so late. It was his own fault that the wheezy village bus would pant off to camp full of other boys but leaving Peter behind.

At the thought of the bus Peter could

bear it no more. The tears filled his eyes. Blindly he continued to jab at the earth with the trowel, but red mud and shaggy weeds and tears seemed all mixed-up together. He wiped at his eyes with his sleeve, a piece of mud brushed off on to

his cheek and the blinding tears still came.

Then a voice said, "And *what* is the matter?"

Peter started. He had not heard Mr. Richards come. He crouched over his trowel still and said, "N-nothing, n-nothing's the matter."

"Nonsense. What's the matter?"

Peter swivelled round on his heels. Mr. Richards' knees were level with his eyes, and just below them it seemed that his trousers ended. They were too short and his ankles showed.

"Stand up," he said crossly. "I can't hear you crouched like that, talking to my feet."

Peter stood up and looked at Mr. Richards' waistcoat instead. Still he did not want to tell what was the matter. He did not even think he knew the words to begin, but once they came it was easy. The story came so fast that the words fell over one another.

"Hm," said Mr. Richards when Peter had finished. "What's the time now?"

"I don't know," Peter said.

"Hm," said Mr. Richards looking at his watch. "Hm, ten to seven. What time does the money have to be in?"

"Seven o'clock," said Peter. "That's the time I have to be home too," he added.

But suddenly he was not crying any more.

"How much money is it that you need?" said Mr. Richards.

"What money?" Peter asked, not trusting the little leap of hope that came to him.

"Your camp money, of course," said Mr. Richards scornfully. "Anyone would think you didn't want it."

"Well," said Peter carefully. "I've got thirteen shillings already, so I still need seven you see, to make the pound."

Mr. Richards fumbled in his trouser pocket, pulling the turn-up on one side even further up his leg. Then he pulled out two half-crowns, a shilling piece, a sixpence, a threepenny bit, two pennies and two halfpennies and held them out to Peter. It made seven shillings exactly.

"But . . ." Peter said, looking in astonishment from Mr. Richards' hand to his white unsmiling face. "But . . ."

"I'm not going to wait all evening, boy," said Mr. Richards. "Take it if you want it. Otherwise I'll keep it for myself. There's plenty I can do with seven shillings."

"But . . ." said Peter again. Then he put out his hand slowly and took the money bit by bit, fumbling with the pennies, and dropping one of the halfpennies on to the rose-bed so that he had to bend and fumble in the earth.

"You needn't think," said Mr. Richards, "that you're getting this for *nothing*." He paused and Peter waited curiously. "In return for this you'll come and weed my garden for an hour every evening for a fortnight and longer if for some *good* reason you cannot come on any evening. You'll be weeding all the time, not cleaning my car again. I shall clean my own car. I do it better. And," he added, "these seven shillings are your wages. You'll get no more than that." He stopped and looked at Peter who was still staring unbelievingly at the money in his hand.

"And if you don't like that plan you can give me my money back."

"But I do like it," said Peter.

"Well, it suits us both, doesn't it?" said Mr. Richards. "You'd give anything on earth to go to your camp and you'll go. I want my garden weeded and I'm getting it done cheap. That suits both of us."

"Yes, oh yes," said Peter. "Thank you, thank you." He smiled all over his face, but still there was nothing on Mr. Richards' face that you could call a smile, and nothing you could call a frown. He was looking at his watch again.

"You'd better *hurry*," he said. "I make it three minutes to seven." Then he added, "Don't run so fast you fall over. I don't need a gardener with broken arms or legs."

Peter had forgotten all his tiredness. Never had he run so fast as he ran down the road now, in spite of Mr. Richards' warning. His full camp fare was clinking and jingling in his pocket. Luckily the headmaster did not live far away, and the clock had only just struck seven by the

time Peter was banging on his cottage door.

"Well, Peter, you've left it rather late, haven't you?" he said when he opened the door and saw Peter standing there, screwing up his pocket to get at the coins. Peter felt one jerk of fright. Was he too late after all? Was one minute too late? But then the headmaster put out his hand, and held it there patiently, waiting.

One by one Peter counted out the sixpences and shillings, the pennies and halfpennies and the fatter half-crowns. There were so many coins that the headmaster's hand was scarcely big enough to hold them all. He had to grab at them quickly with his other hand to save himself dropping any on the doorstep.

Then he looked carefully at the coins, counting them over. Peter held his breath, in case he had made a mistake and not brought enough. At last, the headmaster nodded and turned back indoors, the money clasped tightly in both his hands.

"Good night, Peter," he said. "See you on Monday."

"Good night, sir," said Peter. And he

turned and ran with arms out like an aeroplane for home.

"Brrrr, brrrr . . . I'm a Caravel, I'm a Boeing 707. Brrrrr."

His mother was not cross with him for being late. As soon as she saw Peter the Jet running up the garden path she knew that all was well. She gave him a pleased hug. "Though you're a bad boy, Peter," she said. "You don't deserve a bit of it. Next time you really mustn't leave things so late."

"I won't," said Peter fervently, thinking of the worst parts of his day, like the black-currant-picking.

Lucy was pleased too. She jumped up and down in her dressing-gown, her plaits bumping like skipping-ropes, and sang, "Good old *Peter*, good old *Peter*" to some tune of her own.

But at supper Peter said carelessly and carefully, "Oh, Mum, I'm going to weed Mr. Richards' garden for him the next few evenings. That's all right, isn't it?"

His mother stopped buttering a piece of bread for Lucy and looked at him. Peter felt his face like fire under her gaze. But in a moment she smiled and went back to her buttering.

"Well isn't that good, you'll be able to save your wages for next time," she said.

Peter smiled inside himself. He would not tell her the true story of it. That was a secret between Mr. Richards and himself. He did not look forward to weeding Mr. Richards' garden a bit. But it was easy not to think about that now.

For suddenly he was overcome with everything. There had not been much time before, when he was rushing with the money and then home again. Now all at once he was happy enough to burst. He was too happy even to eat. He had to put down his spoon to give the great grin room to spread into every corner of his face. Everything was all right after all. He was going to camp!